To Casey, Derek, and Rob
—M. S.

For my Dad,
comedy on skates
—Z. P.

Text © 2008 by Marty Sederman.
Illustrations © 2008 by Zachary Pullen.
All rights reserved.

Book design by Amelia May Anderson.
Typeset in Amescote.
The illustrations for this book were rendered in oil on canvas.
Manufactured in China.

Library of Congress Cataloging–in–Publication Data
Sederman, Marty.
Casey and Derek on the ice / by Marty Sederman;
illustrated by Zachary Pullen.
p. cm.
Summary: A rhyming tale of an underdog hockey team's last minute
attempt to win a big game.
ISBN 978-0-8118-5132-9
[1. Hockey—Fiction. 2. Stories in rhyme.] I. Pullen, Zachary, ill. II. Title.
PZ8.3.S445Cas 2008
[E]—dc22
2007021063

10 9 8 7 6 5 4 3 2 1

Chronicle Books LLC
680 Second Street, San Francisco, California 94107

www.chroniclekids.com

CASEY AND DEREK ON THE ICE

BY **Marty Sederman**

ILLUSTRATED BY **Zachary Pullen**

chronicle books · san francisco

The outlook wasn't hopeful for the Rocket team that day,
The score was three to two with just a minute left to play.

So when their left wing stole the puck, the Titans looked convinced
That victory would soon be theirs; this game was surely clinched.

The Titan wing rushed up the side and shot one low and quick.
The Rocket goalie stopped the puck and held it near his stick.

The Rocket fans were cheering when their goalie made the block.
Still, hope was growing dimmer with each second off the clock.

They knew if only Casey and his brother Derek's line
Could quickly get back on the ice, then things would work out fine.

Derek's strength and Casey's speed would get the tying goal.
Any kind of shot would do—"top corner" or "five-hole."

But double shifts had left the brothers tired and worn out.
"Just call for time!" a very eager fan stood up to shout.

The Rockets had no time-out left; they'd used it up before.
They'd clearly need a miracle to even up the score.

Then Casey cleanly won the draw to Derek on his right.
And Derek sprinted down the boards with all his *SPEED* and **MIGHT**.

Then Derek quickly cut "inside," dividing the defense.
The Rocket bench was on its feet and wide-eyed in suspense.

Could Derek beat the goalie? The game came down to this.
He wouldn't get another chance—would Derek score or miss?

The goalie moved out from the net to make the crucial block.
And seconds slowed as everyone awaited Derek's shot.

But Derek's ready hockey stick would never shoot the puck.
A Titan made a desperate lunge, and Derek's skates were struck.

All watched in disbelief as Derek **CRASHED** upon the ice.
He *SLAMMED* into the boards! The final buzzer sounded twice.

The Titans cheered and jumped for joy.
The Rockets had been whipped!
But cheers were quickly muted
when the referees called, **"Tripped!"**

A power play? A penalty shot? What would the refs decide?
The Rockets got a penalty shot, and all their hopes revived.

But Derek couldn't take the shot—he seemed too limp and lame.
So Casey took his place at center ice to tie the game.

The Titan goalie waited in a low and crouching stance.
And Derek's eyes met Casey's in a reassuring glance.

Then Casey skated toward the goal with strides of speed and grace,
A look of sheer determination etched upon his face.

His bearing rang of confidence, no sign of doubt or fear.
He'd dreamed about a chance like this for an entire year.

He head-faked left and cut hard right, and then he let one *FLY*.
The goalie's glove snapped up to stop the puck from getting by.

Then, in that frosty stadium, a team yelled out, **"Hooray!"**
And on that cold and icy rink a hero saved the day.

And one team's fans were smiling as their hearts filled with delight.
They were standing and applauding; Casey's shot went clean "top right."

And so the game was sent into a hard-fought overtime.
The winning goal was scored as soon as Derek joined his line.

Derek *ZIGGED*

and Derek *ZAGGED*

and then he let one rip.

That goalie never had a chance . . .

. . . as in the net it zipped!